The Sea

Illustrated by Ute Fuhr et Raoul Sautai

MOONLIGHT PUBLISHING ❦ FIRST DISCOVERY/Foldouts

The beach at low tide is full of little animals hidden under the sand. Just look how good the birds are at finding where they are and eating them.

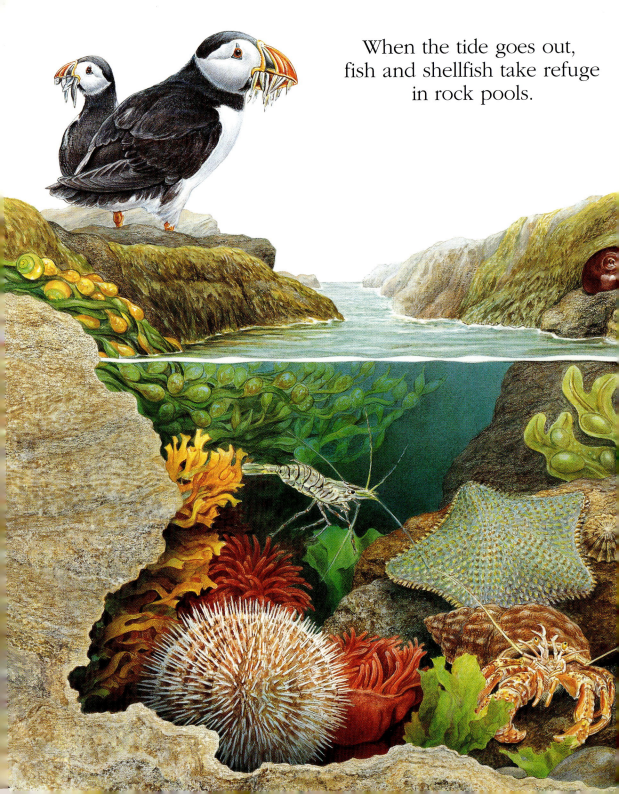

When the tide goes out,
fish and shellfish take refuge
in rock pools.

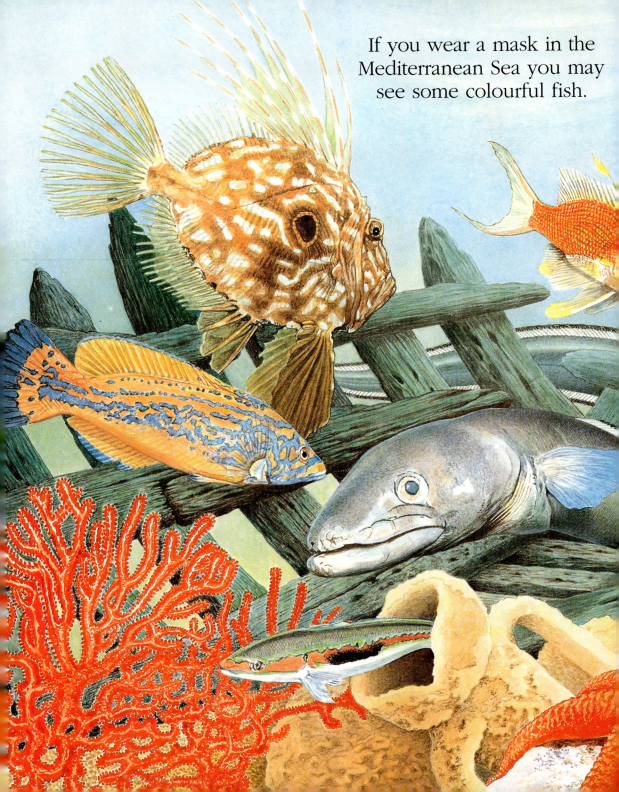

If you wear a mask in the Mediterranean Sea you may see some colourful fish.

Coral reefs enclose a lagoon, in which a multicoloured garden of marine plants grows, and becomes the home to countless fish.

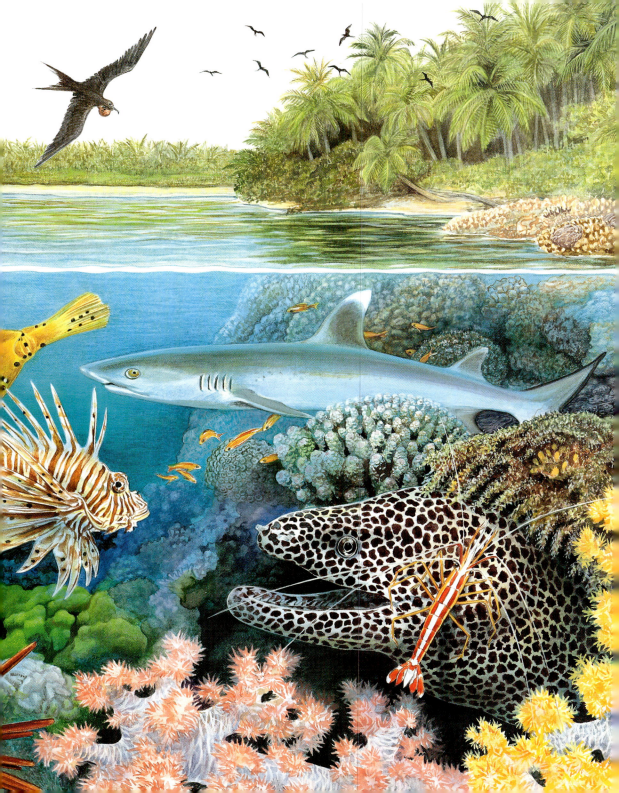

Discover the animals, birds and fish,
which live on the ice-flows
and in the icy seas of the Arctic.

Many fish and marine mammals
make their homes among the foliage
of the giant seaweed forests
of the Pacific Ocean.

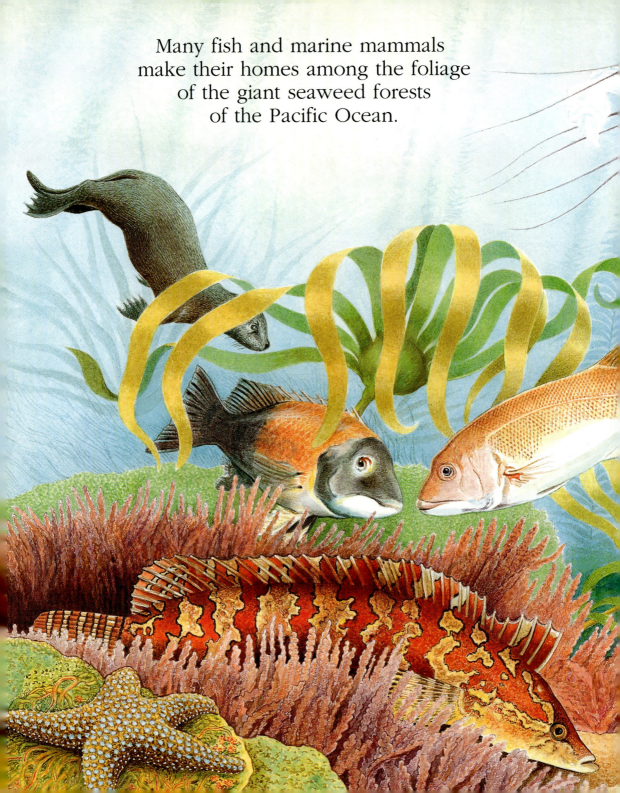

In the depths of the oceans
there is no light at all; animals down
there are covered in luminous dots
which help them to recognize one
another.

Far from the coast you may come across
animals and birds which love the open seas
and can travel fast.

On theses pages you will find some of the
most unusual creatures in the world.

The stone fish is the
most dangerous
because of its poison.

A sea louse comes out of the sea
to lay its eggs on the beach.

The coelacanth is one of the oldest
living creatures on earth.

A white shark has
several rows of
sharp-pointed teeth.

A sawfish has a long upper jaw shaped like a saw.

This seahorse is well disguised with seaweed.

The pygmy goby is the smallest fish of all.

The nautilus has existed for 400 million years.

The leatherback turtle is the largest marine turtle.

. giant manta ray wims along with its nouth open like a iant filter.

The whale shark is the biggest fish of all.

Can you identify all the marine plants fish and animals ...

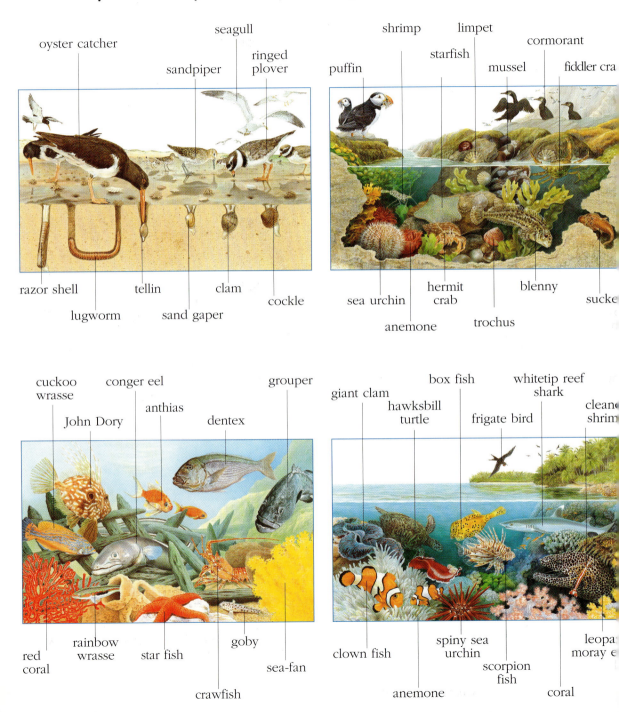

oyster catcher

seagull

sandpiper

ringed plover

shrimp

limpet

starfish

cormorant

puffin

mussel

fiddler cra

razor shell

tellin

clam

cockle

lugworm

sand gaper

sea urchin

hermit crab

blenny

sucke

anemone

trochus

cuckoo wrasse

conger eel

grouper

John Dory

anthias

dentex

red coral

rainbow wrasse

star fish

goby

sea-fan

crawfish

giant clam

box fish

whitetip reef shark

hawksbill turtle

frigate bird

clean shrim

clown fish

spiny sea urchin

scorpion fish

leopa moray e

anemone

coral